Barney's
Christmas Surprise

Dear Parents

Young children love the winter holiday season, especially the tradition of exchanging gifts. In this heart-warming story, BJ and Baby Bop experience the joy of making gifts while learning that giving is as rewarding as receiving.

We consider books to be lifelong gifts that develop and encourage the love of reading. We hope you enjoy reading along with Barney, BJ, and Baby Bop. Happy holidays!

Mary Ann Dudko, Ph.D.
Margie Larsen, M.Ed.
Early Childhood Education Specialists

Art Director: Tricia Legault
Designer: G. Nelson Greenfield

PUFFIN BOOKS

Published by the Penguin Group under licence from Lyons Partnership, L.P.
Penguin Books Ltd, 27 Wrights Lane, London W8 5TZ, England
Penguin Books USA Inc., 375 Hudson Street, New York, New York 10014, USA
Penguin Books Australia Ltd, Ringwood, Victoria, Australia
Penguin Books Canada Ltd, 10 Alcorn Avenue, Toronto, Ontario, Canada M4V 3B2
Penguin Books (NZ) Ltd, 182–190 Wairau Road, Auckland 10, New Zealand

Penguin Books Ltd, Registered Offices: Harmondsworth, Middlesex, England

First published in the USA by Barney™ Publishing, a division of Lyons Partnership, L.P. 1996
Published in Great Britain in Puffin Books 1997
10 9 8 7 6 5 4 3 2 1

Barney's Christmas Surprise

Written by Mark S. Bernthal

Illustrated by Bill Alger

In the kitchen it was warm and cosy! Barney baked biscuits while Baby Bop spread tasty icing on them.

"I can't wait for Christmas!" exclaimed BJ.

"Can we make some of our presents now? Can we?" asked Baby Bop excitedly.

The three friends found special places to work on their presents.
Barney made a wooden truck for BJ.

BJ decorated a sock puppet for Baby Bop.

Baby Bop drew a colourful picture for Barney.

Then they wrapped their Christmas presents in pretty paper, ribbons and bows.

"Oh boy! This box has my name on it!" BJ shouted.

Fresh white snow covered everything.
"The trees look soooo pretty," said Baby Bop.

"The animals look so cold and hungry," said BJ.
"The snow has covered all their food."
Suddenly the three dinosaurs had a
super-dee-duper idea!

Baby Bop made loops for the apples while BJ tied bunches of tasty carrots together. As Barney strung crispy popcorn and plump cranberries together, he chuckled and said, "Oh, this will be such a special Christmas surprise!"

Christmas morning finally arrived.
The sleepy animals awoke to something
wonderful! The squirrels couldn't
believe their eyes.

Barney, BJ, and Baby Bop had decorated a little pine tree with the animals' favourite foods! "Merrrrry Christmas!" shouted the three happy dinosaurs.

Everyone played around the little tree all Christmas morning. Then Baby Bop asked excitedly, "Can we go inside and open our presents now?"

"Thank you, Baby Bop, for the pretty picture," said Barney.

Baby Bop exclaimed, "This is my favourite puppet, BJ! Thanks!"

"You're welcome, Sissy," answered BJ, pushing a new toy. "The truck you made for me is really cool, Barney!"

"It's nice to get special presents,"
said Baby Bop.

"And it's nice to give special presents
too," exclaimed BJ.